MARIGOLD GARDEN

BY KATE GREENAWAY

MARIGOLD GARDEN

·

Pictures and Rhymes

by

KATE GREENAWAY

London
FREDERICK WARNE & CO LTD
& New York
·

You little girl,
You little boy,
With wondering eyes,
That kindly look,
In honour of
Two noble names
I send the offering
Of this book.

Printed in U.S.A.

SUSAN BLUE.

Oh, Susan Blue,
How do you do?
Please may I go for a walk with you?
Where shall we go?
Oh, I know—
Down in the meadow where the cowslips grow!

BLUE SHOES.

LITTLE Blue Shoes
Mustn't go
Very far alone, you know
Else she'll fall down,
Or, lose her way;
Fancy—what
Would mamma say?
Better put her little hand
Under sister's wise command.
When she's a little older grown
Blue Shoes may go quite alone.

STREET SHOW.

Puff, puff, puff. How the trumpets blow
All you little boys and girls come and see
    the show.
One—two—three, the Cat runs up the
    tree;
But the little Bird he flies away—
"She hasn't got me!"

TO THE SUN DOOR.

THEY saw it rise in the morning,
   They saw it set at night,
And they longed to go and see it,
   Ah! if they only might.

The little soft white clouds heard them,
   And stepped from out of the blue;
And each laid a little child softly
   Upon its bosom of dew.

And they carried them higher and higher,
   And they nothing knew any more
Until they were standing waiting
   In front of the round gold door.

And they knocked, and called, and entreated,
   Whoever should be within;
But all to no purpose, for no one
   Would hearken to let them in.

8

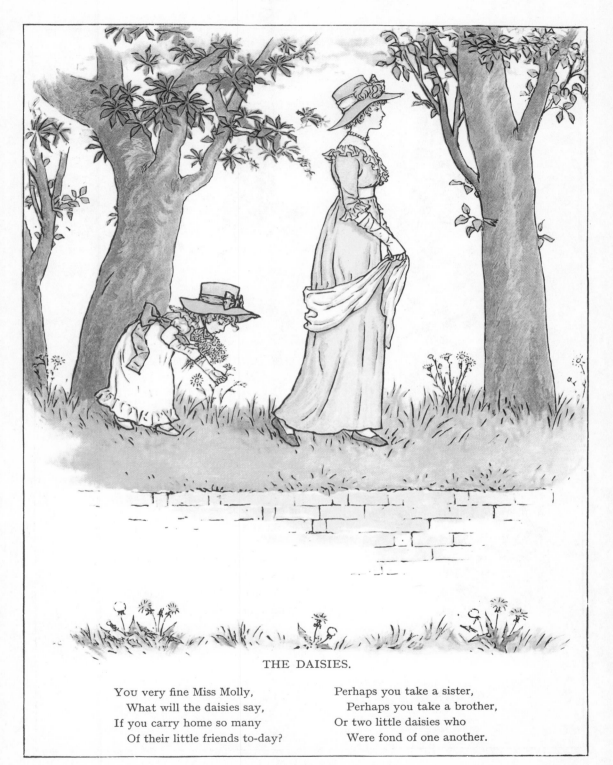

THE DAISIES.

You very fine Miss Molly,
   What will the daisies say,
If you carry home so many
   Of their little friends to-day?

Perhaps you take a sister,
   Perhaps you take a brother,
Or two little daisies who
   Were fond of one another.

THE DANCING FAMILY.

PRAY let me introduce you to
    This little dancing family;
For morning, afternoon, and night
    They danced away so happily.

They twirled round about,
    They turned their toes out;
The people wondered what the noise
    Could all be about.

They danced from early morning,
    Till very late at night;
Both in-doors and out-of-doors,
    With very great delight.

And every sort of dance they knew,
From every country far away;
And so it was no wonder that
They should keep dancing all the day.

So dancing—dancing—dancing,
In sunshine or in rain;
And when they all left off,
Why then—they all began again.

GOING TO SEE GRANDMAMMA.

LITTLE Molly and Damon
  Are walking so far,
For they're going to see
  Their kind Grandmamma.

And they very well know,
  When they get there she'll take
From out of her cupboard
  Some very nice cake.

And into her garden
  They know they may run,
And pick some red currants,
  And have lots of fun.

So Damon to doggie
  Says, "How do you do?"
And asks his mamma
  If he may not go too.

WISHES.

Oh, if you were a little boy,
  And I was a little girl—
Why you would have some whiskers grow
  And then my hair would curl.

Ah! if I could have whiskers grow,
  I'd let you have my curls;
But what's the use of wishing it—
  Boys never can be girls.

FIRST ARRIVALS.

It is a Party, do you know,
And there they sit, all in a row,
Waiting till the others come,
To begin to have some fun.

Hark! the bell rings sharp and clear,
Other little friends appear;
And no longer all alone
They begin to feel at home.

To them a little hard is Fate,
Yet better early than too late;
Fancy getting there forlorn,
With the tea and cake all gone.

Wonder what they'll have for tea;
Hope the jam is strawberry.
Wonder what the dance and game;
Feel so very glad they came.

Very Happy may you be,
May you much enjoy your tea.

KG.

WHEN WE WENT OUT WITH GRANDMAMMA.

WHEN we went out with Grandmamma—
   Mamma said for a treat—
Oh, dear, how stiff we had to walk
   As we went down the street.

One on each side we had to go,
   And never laugh or loll;
I carried Prim, her Spaniard dog,
   And Tom—her parasol.

If *I* looked right—*if Tom* looked left—
   "Tom—Susan—I'm ashamed;
And little Prim, I'm sure, is shocked,
   To hear such naughties named."

She said we had no manners,
   If we ever talked or sung;
"You should have seen," said Grandmamma,
   "*Me* walk, when *I* was young."

She said they never wished then
   To play—oh, indeed!
They learnt to sew and needlework,
   Or else to write and read.

She told us—oh, so often—
   How little girls and boys,
In the good days when she was young,
   Never made any noise.

She said her mother never let
   Her speak a word at meals;
"But now," said Grandmamma, "you'd think
   That children's tongues had wheels

"So fast they go—clack, clack, clack, clack;
   Now listen well, I pray,
And let me see you both improve
   From what I've said to-day."

TO MYSTERY LAND.

Oʜ, dear, how will it end?
Peggy and Susie how naughty
　　you are.
You little know where you are,
Going so far, and so high,
Nearly up to the sky.
Perhaps it's a Giant who
　　lives there,
And perhaps it's a lovely
　　Princess.
But you very well know
You've no business to go;
You'll get yourselves into a mess.

Oh, dear, I'm sure it is true;
Whatever on earth can it matter
　　to you?
For you know it—oh, fie—
That it's naughty to pry
Into other's affairs—
Into other folks houses to go,
Where you know
You're not asked.
So you'd better come back
While there's time, it is plain.
Go home—and be never
So naughty again.

FROM MARKET.

OH who'll give us Posies,
And Garlands of Roses,
To twine round our heads so gay?
For here we come bringing
You many good wishes to-day.
From market—from market—from market—
We all come up from market.

LITTLE PHILLIS.

I AM a very little girl,
　　I think that I've turned two;
And if you'd like to know my name
　　I'd like to tell it you.

They always call me Baby,
　　But Phillis is my name.
No—no one ever gave it me,
　　I think it only came.

I've got a pretty tulip
　　In my little flower-bed;
If you would like I'll give it you—
　　It's yellow, striped with red.

I've got a little kitten, but
　　I can't give that away,
She likes to play with me *so* much;
　　She's gone to sleep to-day.

And I've got a nice new dolly,
　　Shall I fetch her out to you?
She's got such pretty shoes on,
　　And her bonnet's trimmed with blue.

You'd like to take her home with you?
　　Oh, *no*, she mustn't go;
Good-bye—I want to run now,
　　You walk along so slow.

THE FOUR PRINCESSES.

FOUR Princesses lived in a Green Tower—
  A Bright Green Tower in the middle of the
    sea;
And no one could think—oh, no one could
    think—
  Who the Four Princesses could be.

One looked to the North, and one to the South,
  And one to the East, and one to the West;
They were all so pretty, so very pretty,
  You could not tell which was the prettiest.

Their curls were golden—their eyes were blue,
  And their voices were sweet as a silvery bell;
And four white birds around them flew,
  But where they came from—*who* could tell?

Oh, who could tell? for no one knew,
  And not a word could you hear them say.
But the sound of their singing, like church bells ringing,
  Would sweetly float as they passed away.

For under the sun, and under the stars,
  They often sailed on the distant sea;
Then in their Green Tower and Roses bower
  They lived again—a mystery.

WHEN YOU AND I GROW UP.

WHEN you and I
Grow up—Polly—
　　I mean that you and me,
Shall go sailing in a big ship
　　Right over all the sea.
We'll wait till we are older,
　　For if we went to-day,
You know that we might lose ourselves,
　　And never find the way.

IN AN APPLE TREE.

In September, when the apples were red,

To Belinda I said,

"Would you like to go away

To Heaven, or stay

Here in this orchard full of trees

All your life?" And she said, "If you please

I'll stay here—where I know,

And the flowers grow."

THE WEDDING BELLS.

THE Wedding Bells were ringing,
　And Monday was the day,
And all the little ladies
　Were there so fresh and gay.

And up—up—up the steps they went,
　The wedding fine to see;
And the Roses were all for the Bride,
　So pretty—so pretty was she.

THE LITTLE LONDON GIRL.

In my little Green House, quite content am I,
When the hot sun pours down from the sky;
For oh, I love the country—the beautiful country.
Who'd live in a London street when there's the country?

I live in a London street, then I long and long
To be the whole day the sweet Flowers among
Instead of tall chimney-pots up in the sky,
The joy of seeing Birds and Dragon Flies go by.

At home I lie in bed, and cannot go to sleep,
For the sound of cart-wheels upon the hard street.
But here my eyes close up to no sound of anything
Except it is to hear the nightingales sing.

And then I see the Chickens and the Geese go walking,
I hear the Pigs and the Ducks all talking.
And the Red and the Spotted Cows they stare at me,
As if they wondered whoever I could be.

I see the little Lambs out with their mothers—
Such pretty little white young sisters and brothers.
Oh, I'll stay in the country, and make a daisy chain,
And never go back to London again.

TO BABY.

Oh, what shall my blue eyes go see?
  Shall it be pretty Quack-Quack to-day?
Or the Peacock upon the Yew Tree?
  Or the dear little white Lambs at play?
        Say Baby.
For Baby is such a young Petsy,
  And Baby is such a sweet Dear.
And Baby is growing quite old now—
  She's just getting on for a year.

WILLY AND HIS SISTER.

Willy said to his sister,
    "Please may I go with you?"
She said, "You must behave
    Very nicely if you do."

"Please will you take me then
    To look at the mill?"
"Yes," she said, "because you are
    So very good—I will."

"The miller he is
    So very white and kind;
And sprinkled all over
    With the flour they grind.

"And the big heaps of corn
    That lie upon the floor;
He will let me play with those
    I am quite sure.

"I like to hear the wheel
    Make such a rushing sound,
And see the pretty water
    Go round, and round, and round

"So take me to the mill,
    For then you shall see
What a very, very good boy
    I really mean to be."

AT SCHOOL.

Five little Girls, sitting on a form,
Five little Girls, with lessons to learn,
Five little Girls, who, I'm afraid,
Won't know them a bit when they have to be said.

For little eyes are given to look
Anywhere else than on their book;
And little thoughts are given to stray
Anywhere—ever so far away.

HAPPY DAYS.

"ARE you going next week to see Phillis and Phoebe?
    Phillis on Monday will be just fourteen.
She says we shall all have our tea in the garden,
    And afterwards have some nice games on the green.

"I wanted a new frock, but mother said, 'No,'
    So I must be content with my old one you see.
But then white is so pretty, and kind Aunt Matilda
    Has sent down a beautiful necklace for me."

"Oh, yes, I am going, and Peggy is going,
　　And mother is making us new frocks to wear;
I shall have my red sash and my hat with pink ribbons—
　　I know all the girls will be smart who are there.

"And then, too, we're going to each take a nosegay—
　　The larger the better—for Phillis to say
That all her friends love her, and wish her so happy,
　　And bring her sweet flowers upon her birthday.

"And won't it be lovely, in beautiful sunshine,
　　The table spread under the great apple tree,
To see little Phillis—that dear little Phillis—
　　Look smiling all round as she pours out the tea!"

THE LITTLE QUEEN'S COMING.

WITH Roses—red Roses,
We'll pelt her with Roses,
And Lilies—white Lilies we'll drop at
her feet;
The little Queen's coming,
The people are running—
The people are running to greet and
to meet.

Then clash out a welcome,
Let all the bells sound, come,
To give her a welcoming proud and
sweet.
How her blue eyes will beam,
And her golden curls gleam,
When the sound of our singing rings
down the street.

ON THE WALL TOP.

Dancing and prancing to town we go,
On the top of the wall of the town we go.
Shall we talk to the stars, or talk to the moon,
Or run along home to our dinner so soon?

ON THE WALL TOP.

So high—so high on the wall we run,
The nearer the sky—why, the nearer the sun,
If you give me one penny, I'll give you two,
For that's the way good neighbours do.

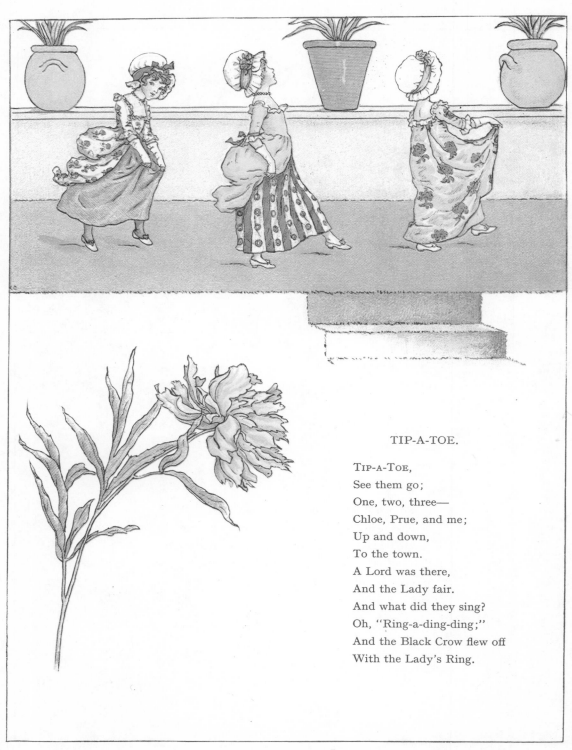

TIP-A-TOE.

TIP-A-TOE,
See them go;
One, two, three—
Chloe, Prue, and me;
Up and down,
To the town.
A Lord was there,
And the Lady fair.
And what did they sing?
Oh, "Ring-a-ding-ding;"
And the Black Crow flew off
With the Lady's Ring.

MAMMAS AND BABIES.

"My Polly is so very good,
　Belinda never cries;
My Baby often goes to sleep,
　See how she shuts her eyes.

"Dear Mrs. Lemon tell me when
　Belinda goes to school;
And what time does she go to bed?"
"Well, eight o'clock's the rule.

"But now and then, just for a treat,
　I let her wait awhile;
You shake your head—why, wouldn't
　　　you?
　Do look at Baby's smile!"

"Dear Mrs. Primrose will you come
　　One day next week to tea?
　　Of course bring Rosalinda, and
　　　That darling—Rosalie."

"Dear Mrs. Cowslip, you *are* kind;
　　My little folks, I know,
　Will be so very pleased to come;
　　Dears—tell Mrs. Cowslip so.

"Oh, do you know—perhaps you've not
　　　heard—
　　She had a dreadful fright;
　My Daisy with the measles
　　Kept me up every night.

"And then I've been so worried—
　　Clarissa had a fit;
　And the doctor said he couldn't
　　In the least account for it."

MY LITTLE GIRLIE.

LITTLE girlie tell to me
What your wistful blue eyes see?
Why you like to stand so high,
Looking at the far off sky.

Does a tiny Fairy flit
In the pretty blue of it?
Or is it that you hope so soon
To see the rising yellow Moon?

Or is it—as I think I've heard—
You're looking for a little Bird
To come and sit upon a spray,
And sing the summer night away?

THE CATS HAVE COME TO TEA.

WHAT did she see—oh, what did she see,
As she stood leaning against the tree?
Why all the Cats had come to tea.

What a fine turn out—from round about,
All the houses had let them out,
And here they were with scamper and shout.

"Mew—mew—mew!" was all they could say,
And, "We hope we find you well to-day."

Oh, what should she do—oh, what should she do?
What a lot of milk they would get through;
For here they were with "Mew—mew—mew!"

She didn't know—oh, she didn't know,
If bread and butter they'd like or no;
They might want little mice, oh! oh! oh!

Dear me—oh, dear me,
All the cats had come to tea.

THE TEA PARTY.

In the pleasant green Garden
  We sat down to tea;
"Do you take sugar?" and
  "Do you take milk?"
She'd got a new gown on—
  A smart one of silk.
We all were so happy
  As happy could be,
On that bright Summer's day
  When she asked us to tea.

UNDER ROSE ARCHES.

UNDER Rose Arches to Rose Town—
    Rose Town on the top of the hill;
For the Summer wind blows and music goes,
    And the violins sound shrill.

Oh, Roses shall be for her carpet,
    And her curtains of Roses so fair;
And a Rosy crown, while far adown
    Floats her long golden hair.

Twist and twine Roses and Lilies,
    And little leaves green,
    Fit for a queen;
Twist and twine Roses and Lilies.

Twist and twine Roses and Lilies,
    And all the bells ring,
    And all the people sing;
Twist and twine Roses and Lilies.

A GENTEEL FAMILY.

SOME children are so naughty,
   And some are very good;
But the Genteel Family
   Did always what it should.

They put on gloves when they went out.
   And ran not in the street;
And on wet days not one of them
   Had ever muddy feet.

Then they were always so polite,
   And always thanked you so;
And never threw their toys about,
   As naughty children do.

KG

They always learnt their lessons
    When it was time they should;
And liked to eat up all their crusts—
    They were so very good.

And then their frocks were never torn,
    Their tuckers always clean;
And their hair so very tidy—
    Always quite fit to be seen.

Then they made calls with their mamma
    And were so very neat;
And learnt to bow becomingly
    When they met you in the street.

And really they were everything
    That children ought to be;
And well may be examples now
    For little you—and me.

BABY MINE.

BABY mine, over the trees;
  Baby mine, over the flowers;
Baby mine, over the sunshine;
  Baby mine, over the showers.

Baby mine, over the land;
  Baby mine, over the water.
Oh, when had a mother before
  Such a sweet—such a sweet, little daughter!

LITTLE GIRLS AND LITTLE LAMBS.

In the May-time flowers grow;
Little girls in meadows go;
Little lambs frisk with delight,
And in the green grass sleep at night.
Little birds sing all the day,
Oh, in such a happy way!
All the day the sun is bright,
Little stars shine all the night.
The Cowslip says to the Primrose,
"How soft the little Spring wind blows!"
The Daisy and the Buttercup
Sing every time that they look up.
For beneath the sweet blue sky
They see a pretty Butterfly;
The Butterfly, when he looks down,
Says, "What a pretty Flower Town!"

FROM WONDER WORLD.

OUT of Wonder World I think you
　　come;
For in your eyes the wonder comes
　　with you.
The stars are the windows of Heaven,
And sometimes I think you peep
　　through.
Oh, little girl, tell us do the Flowers
Tell you secrets when they find you
　　all alone?
Or the Birds and Butterflies whisper
Of things to us unknown?

Or do angel voices speak to you so softly,
When *we* only hear a little wind sigh;
And the peaceful dew of Heaven fall upon you
When *we* only see a white cloud passing by?

CHILD'S SONG.

THE King and the Queen were riding
   Upon a Summer's day,
And a Blackbird flew above them,
   To hear what they did say.

The King said he liked apples,
   The Queen said she liked pears.
And what shall we do to the Blackbird
   Who listens unawares.

MISS MOLLY AND THE LITTLE FISHES.

OH, sweet Miss Molly,
You're so fond
Of Fishes in a little Pond.
And perhaps they're glad
To see you stare
With such bright eyes
Upon them there.
And when your fingers and your thumbs
Drop slowly in the small white crumbs
I hope they're happy.   Only this—
When you've looked long enough, sweet miss.
Then, most beneficent young giver,
Restore them to their native river.

THE LITTLE JUMPING GIRLS.

Jump—jump—jump—
  Jump away
From this town into
  The next, to-day.

Jump—jump—jump—
  Jump over the moon;
Jump all the morning,
  And all the noon.

Jump—jump—jump—
　　Jump all night;
Won't our mothers
　　Be in a fright?

Jump—jump—jump—
　　Over the sea;
What wonderful wonders
　　We shall see.

Jump—jump—jump—
　　And leave behind
Everything evil
　　That we may find.

Jump—jump—jump—
　　Jump far away;
And all come home
　　Some other day.

RING-A-RING.

Ring-a-ring of little boys.
Ring-a-ring of girls;
All around—all around,
Twists and twirls.

You are merry children;
"Yes, we are."
Where do you come from?
"Not very far.

"We live in the mountain,
We live in the tree;
And I live in the river-bed,
And you won't catch me!"

ON THE BRIDGE.

IF I could see a little fish—
That is what I just now wish!
I want to see his great round eyes
Always open in surprise.

I wish a water rat would glide
Slowly to the other side;
Or a dancing spider sit
On the yellow flags a bit.

I think I'll get some stones to throw,
And watch the pretty circles show.
Or shall we sail a flower-boat,
And watch it slowly—slowly float?

That's nice—because you never know
How far away it means to go;
And when to-morrow comes, you see,
It may be in the great wide sea.

BALL.

ONE—two, is one to you:
One—two—three, is one to me.
Throw it fast or not at all,
And mind you do not let it fall.

Fairy Blue Eyes
    And Fairy Brown,
And dear little Golden Curls,
    Look down.
I say "Good-bye"—
    "Good-bye" with no pain—
Till some happy day
    We meet again!

Original wood block designs engraved by
Edmund Evans Limited